ie!
ng
Grove!
Love,
Grammy
&
Grampy

The Perfect Place

Story by Stephanie Turcotte Edenholm
Illustrated by D.J. Jackson

One morning in late September, Mozzie prepared her antennae to smell out some flowers and get a tasty treat of nectar. But something out of the ordinary caught her attention.

Mozzie noticed that several of her monarch
friends were already out flying; however, they
weren't collecting nectar. They were leaving
the milkweed fields of Spirit Lake!

As Mozzie landed on a nectar-rich penstemon, she spotted her friend Mack. He flew toward her as if he were on a very important mission.

She asked, "Where are you going in such a hurry Mack? And where are *they* going?" She looked in the direction of the monarchs who were flying away.

"Don't you know? It's time!" Mack said.

Mozzie saw Mack's wings flap and knew he was going to fly away, so she quickly asked, "Time for what?"

Mack replied, "Time to go south!"

And just as abruptly as he appeared, he was gone again.

Several days passed, and Mozzie watched curiously as her monarch friends left Spirit Lake. After sucking up the last drop of coneflower nectar through her proboscis, Mozzie decided to head off. She flew off in the same southwest direction as her friend Mack and the others. Maybe, if she followed them, she would figure out why the monarchs were leaving and where they were going.

Mozzie felt like she had been flying for many
hours that day. She had no idea that she
flew one-hundred miles. Mozzie drank from
different delicious flowers along the way.
Although she saw other monarchs from time
to time, she never saw Mack.

Late in the afternoon, the sun's intensity faded, and the temperature fell below fifty-five degrees. Mozzie felt a familiar feeling as her muscles stiffened. She looked for a safe place to land and fold her wings for the evening.

Suddenly, Mozzie noticed a beautiful ponderosa pine. One branch was decorated with about fifteen monarchs.

What a nice cluster, she thought. Although she didn't recognize any of the butterflies, it felt so much better to be with other monarchs than to be alone.

Mozzie stayed for the night.

As the sun warmed her the next morning, Mozzie gently flapped her wings. A few of the monarchs hanging on the upper branch were already flying off. Before Mozzie knew it, she was the only monarch left on the great ponderosa pine tree. She felt hungry, so she used her antennae to smell for more nectar.

Mozzie's routine was the same for seven or eight more days. She flew many hours and many miles. Sometimes she stopped and filled her abdomen with tasty nectar. And every afternoon she found a cluster of monarchs and spent the night with them. Sometimes twenty monarchs or more were in the cluster, and other times only five or six.

Mozzie had not found Mack. She also had not figured out why all the monarchs left Spirit Lake, or why they were headed southwest.

On her tenth day of traveling, Mozzie was worn out. She did not want to fly over another field, stream, tree, road, or house. She heard a familiar voice echo from a tall Monterey pine tree. "Eureka! We've struck gold!" exclaimed Mack. Mozzie flew as fast as she could to her friend to find out what the commotion was all about.

Mozzie found Mack slurping up a huge water droplet on the end of a green pine needle. She forgot all about the excitement of finding her friend. Mozzie asked, "What do you mean *we struck gold*?" Mozzie realized Mack was not surprised to see her because he continued to drink droplets.

He finished slurping and replied, "Look at this place. It's perfect!"

Mozzie looked around. She thought it was a nice place, but she had seen many nice places along her journey from Spirit Lake. "What makes this place so perfect, Mack?" she asked.

Mack said, "First of all, the temperature here is just right. Not too hot, not too cold. It's like a refrigerator, not a freezer. And did you see the size of that water droplet I just drank? They are all over the place—on the leaves of the trees and dangling from the ends of the pine needles like liquid jewels."

"Let me ask you a question, Mozzie. Aren't you tired of getting tossed around by the wind?"

Mozzie thought about her long journey and said, "Yes, it did get a little rough at times. Actually, I have a small tear in my forewing."

"Precisely! Now look around," Mack instructed, "Look at all these trees! Some are short, some are tall, and they all have branches at different heights. The trees protect us from the wind. We can also move up and down the trees to catch the light of the sun." Mozzie looked around and understood what Mack wanted her to be excited about. She also noticed beautiful beams of light filtering through the branches and the fog.

Mozzie flew to a nearby cypress branch that hung over a walking path. She joined several other monarchs who spread their wings wide open, enjoying the last bit of afternoon sun. Mack said, "And look over there—a flowering daisy bush. We even have nectar here!"

Mozzie said, "I'm not hungry, Mack. I ate enough on my way here. I may not need to eat for months."

Mack said, "Well, the nectar is here if you need it. My mind is made up. This is the perfect place, and I am going to stay right here." Mack took a spot next to Mozzie on the branch and opened up his wings as if to catch a splash of sun. Mozzie took in a happy breath and made herself at home.

Mozzie stayed in the area for several weeks, investigating and exploring. Mack was right. This was the perfect place. It seemed that all the other monarchs agreed because as the month passed, more and more monarchs arrived. And few, if any, ever left. Mozzie had never seen so many monarchs in one spot. First there were hundreds, and then there were thousands.

Every night, thousands and thousands of monarchs hung together from the branches of the trees like shingles on a roof.

People of different sizes, shapes, and colors came to visit the perfect place as well.

Mozzie heard them call the special place a *sanctuary*.

In February, five months after Mozzie arrived at the sanctuary, she noticed a curious kind of monarch behavior. She saw games of chase. Mozzie flew over to ask the expert. "Mack, now what's going on?"

Mack said, "It's mating season. And it's almost time for you to leave."

Mozzie was confused. "What do you mean, leave? I think this is the perfect place."

Mack said, "It was the perfect place to spend the winter. Now it's spring, and you have to go out and find milkweed so you can lay your eggs."

"Don't we have milkweed here?" Mozzie asked.

"Not here. You have to go to the fields in the valleys where it grows," Mack said.

Mozzie asked,
"How many eggs
will I lay?"

Mack replied, "Possibly 400 eggs."

"Wow! That's so much work," Mozzie exclaimed.

"Yes, but just think. You alone could be responsible for 400 new monarchs." Mack zipped off to find a snack of nectar.

The thought of 400 new monarchs flying around made Mozzie very happy.

While Mack gathered nectar from a nearby bottlebrush bloom, Mozzie thought seriously about what Mack had told her. She flew over to him and said, "Well, I have decided that laying 400 eggs is very important work. We definitely need more monarchs."

Mozzie waited for Mack to flap his wings in agreement. He was looking away at two or three female monarchs who flew by. Then he finally moved his wings up and down, and she knew he agreed.

"Good-bye, Mack. I'm off to do my part. Thanks for all your help!" Mozzie yelled as a male monarch sped her way.

At the end of February, Mozzie left the perfect place in search of milkweed so that she could lay her eggs. She found a large field of milkweed in the Central Valley of California.

Mozzie carefully laid a single egg on each milkweed plant to make sure that every one of her children had enough to eat.

Mozzie even went as far as the Sierra foothills to successfully lay the last of her eggs. She hoped all her eggs would change and emerge into beautiful male and female monarchs. It would not be her children or her grandchildren who would make the migration the next fall. Those generations would make their way north following the natural cycle of milkweed. She was sure that next October her great-great- grandchildren would find a perfect place along the California coast.

Maybe they would even find her *perfect place* in Pacific Grove, California.

Did You Know?

1. The Summer generations of the monarch butterfly typically live 4 to 6 weeks.

2. Overwintering monarchs, like Mozzie and Mack, can live between 6 to 8 months.

3. When a monarch caterpillar eats milkweed, it makes the monarch toxic to its predators.

4. The bright colors of the monarch caterpillar and butterfly are a warning to predators to leave them alone. They don't taste good, and can make predators sick.

5. Monarch anatomy
   - Six legs, like other insects, and feet for tasting
   - two antennae to help it stay balanced and to smell
   - a straw-like tube (proboscis) for drinking nectar and water
   - two compound eyes

6. You can help Monarchs by planting nectar-producing flowers in your garden. If you don't live within 10 miles of an overwintering site, like Pacific Grove, then you can plant native milkweed plants to give female monarchs, like Mozzie, the necessary plants to lay their eggs.

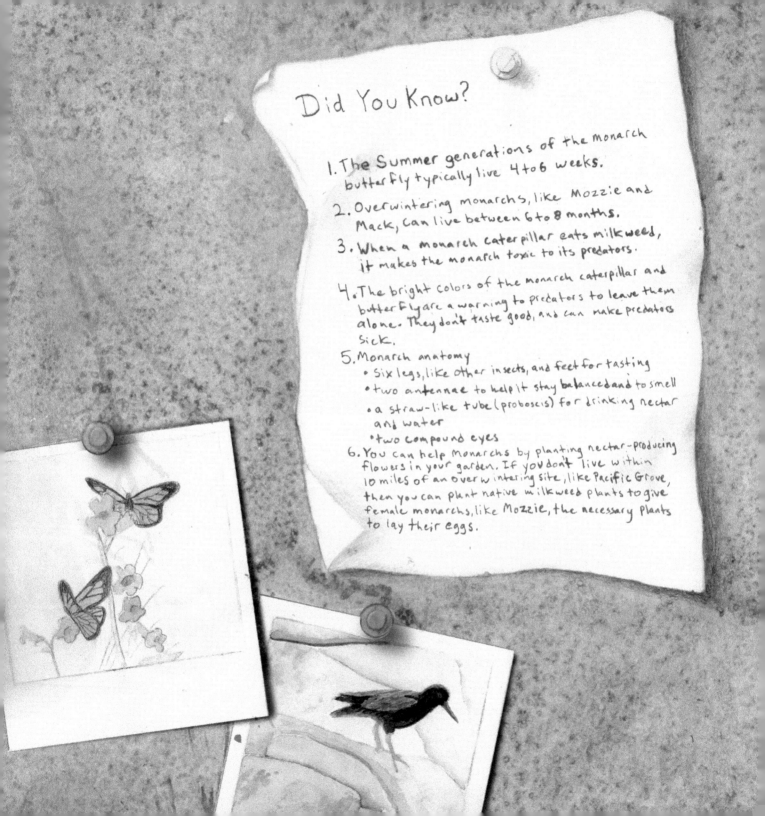

Second edition
ISBN: 978-1-0879-6064-7 (hardcover)
ISBN: 978-1-0878-8147-8 (softcover)

First published by Dog Ear Publishing

CPSIA information can be obtained
at www.ICGtesting.com
Printed in the USA
BVHW062255280922
648259BV00003B/32